PUFFIN BOOKS
GETTING GRANNY'S GLASSES

Born in Kasauli (Himachal Pradesh) in 1934, Ruskin Bond grew up in Jamnagar (Gujarat), Dehradun, New Delhi and Simla. His first novel *The Room on the Roof,* written when he was seventeen, received the John Llewellyn Rhys Memorial Prize in 1957. Since then he has written over five hundred short stories, essays and novellas (some included in the collections *Dust on the Mountains* and *Classic Ruskin Bond*) and more than forty books for children. He received the Sahitya Akademi Award for English writing in India in 1993, the Padma Shri in 1999, and the Delhi government's Lifetime Achievement Award in 2012. He has now been awarded the Sahitya Akademi's Bal Sahitya Puraskar for his 'total contribution to children's literature'.

He lives in Landour, Mussoorie, with his extended family.

ALSO IN PUFFIN BY RUSKIN BOND

RUSKIN BOND

Getting Granny's Glasses

Illustrated by
Sayantan Halder

PUFFIN BOOKS
An imprint of Penguin Random House

PUFFIN BOOKS

USA | Canada | UK | Ireland | Australia
New Zealand | India | South Africa | China

Puffin Books is part of the Penguin Random House group of companies
whose addresses can be found at global.penguinrandomhouse.com

Published by Penguin Random House India Pvt. Ltd
4th Floor, Capital Tower 1, MG Road,
Gurugram 122 002, Haryana, India

Penguin
Random House
India

First published by Julia MacRae Books in the UK 1985
First published in India in Puffin by Penguin Books 2012

Text Copyright @ Ruskin Bond 1985
Illustrations copyright@ Sayantan Halder 2012

37

ISBN 9780143332466

Typeset in Sabon
Printed at :Aarvee Promotions India

www.penguin.co.in

Chapter One

Granny could hear the distant roar of the river, and smell the pine needles beneath her feet, and feel the presence of her grandson, Mani. But she couldn't see the river or the trees; and of her grandson she could only make out his fuzzy hair, and sometimes, when he was very close, his blackberry eyes and the gleam of his teeth when he smiled.

1

Granny wore a pair of old glasses; she'd been wearing them for well over ten years, but her eyes had grown steadily weaker, and the glasses had grown older. They were now scratched and spotted, and there was very little she could see through them. Still, they were better than nothing. Without them, everything was just a topsy-turvy blur.

Of course Granny knew her way about the house and the fields, and on a clear day she could see the mountains—the mighty Himalayan snow peaks—striding away into the sky; but it was felt by Mani and his father that it was high time Granny had her eyes tested and got herself new glasses.

'Well, you know we can't get them in the village,' said Granny.

Mani said, 'You'll have to go to the eye hospital in Mussoorie. That's the nearest town.'

'But that's a two-day journey,' protested Granny. 'First I'd have to walk to Nain market, twelve miles at least, spend the night there at your uncle's place, and then catch a bus for the rest of the journey! You know how I hate buses. And it's ten years since I walked all the way to Mussoorie. That was when I had *these* glasses made.'

'Well, it's still there,' said Mani's father.

'What is?'

'Mussoorie.'

'And the eye hospital?'

'That too.'

'Well, my eyes are not too bad, really,' said Granny, looking for excuses. She did not feel like going far from the village; in particular she did not want to be parted from Mani. He was eleven and quite capable of looking after himself, but Granny had brought him up ever since his mother had died when he was only a year old. She was his Nani (maternal grandmother), and had cared for boy and father, cows and hens, and the household all these years, with great energy and devotion. Even her failing eyesight hadn't prevented her from milking cows or preparing meals or harvesting the corn.

'I can manage quite well,' she said. 'As
long as I can see what's right in front of me,
there's no problem. I know you've got a ball
in your hand, Mani. Please don't bounce it
off the cow.'

'It's not a ball, Granny, it's an apple.'

'Oh, is it?' said Granny, recovering quickly from her mistake. 'Never mind. Just don't bounce it off the cow. And don't eat too many apples!'

Chapter Two

'Now listen,' said Mani's father sternly.
'I know you don't want to go anywhere.
But we're not sending you off on your own.
I'll take you to Mussoorie.'

'And leave Mani here by himself? How
could you even think of doing that?'

'Then I'll take you to Mussoorie,' said
Mani eagerly. 'We can leave Father on his
own, can't we? I've been to Mussoorie before,
with my school friends. I know where we can
stay. But. . .' He paused a moment and looked
doubtfully from his father to his grandmother.
'You wouldn't be able to walk all the way to
Nain, would you Granny?'

'Of course I can walk,' replied Granny.
'I may be going blind, but there's nothing
wrong with my legs!'

That was true enough. Only the day before
they'd found Granny in the walnut tree,
tossing walnuts, not very accurately, into
a large basket on the ground.

'But you're nearly seventy, Granny,' said
Mani.

'What has that got to do with it? And
besides, it's downhill to Nain.'

'And uphill coming back,' Mani reminded.

'Uphill's easier!' said Granny. Now that she knew Mani might be accompanying her, she was more than ready to make the journey.

The monsoon rains had begun, and in front of the small stone house a cluster of giant dahlias reared their heads. Mani had seen them growing in Nain and had brought some bulbs home.

'These are big flowers, Granny,' he'd said. 'You'll be able to see them better.'

And she could indeed see the dahlias, splashes of red and yellow against the old stone of the cottage walls.

Looking at them now, Granny said, 'While we're in Mussoorie we'll get some seeds and bulbs. And a new bell for the white cow. And a pullover for your father. And shoes for you—look, there's nothing much left of the ones you're wearing.'

'Now just a minute,' interrupted Mani's father. 'Are you going there to have your eyes tested, or are you going on a shopping expedition? I've got only a hundred rupees to spare. You'll have to manage with that.'

'We'll manage,' said Mani. 'We'll sleep at the bus shelter.'

'No, we won't,' said Granny. 'I've got fifty rupees of my own. We'll stay in a hotel!'

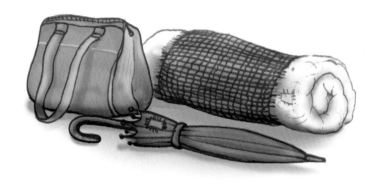

Chapter Three

Early next morning, in a light drizzle, Granny and Mani set out on the path to Nain.

Mani carried a small bedding roll on his shoulder; Granny carried a large cloth shopping bag and an umbrella.

The path went through fields and around the brow of the hill and then began to wind here and there, up and down and around, as though it had a will of its own and no intention of going anywhere in particular. Travellers new to the area often left the path, because they were impatient or in a hurry, and thought there were quicker, better ways of reaching their destinations. Almost immediately they found themselves lost. For it was a wise path and a good path, and had found the right way of crossing the mountains after centuries of trial and error.

'Whenever you feel tired, we'll take rest,' said Mani.

'We've only just started out,' said Granny. 'We'll rest when you're hungry!'

They walked at a steady pace, without talking too much. A flock of parrots whirled overhead, flashes of red and green against the sombre sky. High in a spruce tree a barbet called monotonously. But there were no other sounds, except for the hiss and gentle patter of the rain.

Mani stopped to pick wild blackberries from a bush. Granny wasn't fond of berries and did not slacken her pace. Mani had to run to catch up with her. Soon his lips were purple with the juice from the berries.

The rain stopped and the sun came out. Below them, the light green of the fields stood out against the dark green of the forests, and the hills were bathed in golden sunshine.

Mani ran ahead a little.

'Can you see all right, Granny?' he called.

'I can see the path and I can see your white shirt. That's enough for just now.'

'Well, watch out, there are some mules coming down the road,' warned Mani.

Granny stepped aside to allow the mules to pass. They clattered by, the mule-driver urging them on with a romantic song; but the last mule veered towards Granny and appeared to be heading straight for her. Granny saw it in time. She knew that mules and ponies always preferred going *round* objects, if they could see what lay ahead of them, so she held out her open umbrella

and the mule cantered round it without touching her.

Poor mule, thought Granny, as she hurried after Mani. Perhaps it needs glasses too.

They ate their lunch on the roadside, in the shade of a whispering pine. There were chapatties and mango pickle, and a curry made from yams. They drank from a spring a little further down the path.

By late afternoon they were directly above Nain.

'We're almost there,' said Mani. 'I can see the temple near Raju Uncle's house.'

'I can't see a thing,' said Granny.

'That's because of the mist. There's a thick mist coming up the valley.'

It began raining heavily as they entered the small market town on the banks of the river. Granny's umbrella was leaking badly. But they were soon drying themselves in Raju Uncle's house, and drinking glasses of hot, sweet milky tea.

Mani got up early next morning and ran down the narrow street to bathe in the river. The swift but shallow mountain river was a tributary of the sacred Ganges, and its waters were held sacred too. As the sun rose,

people thronged the steps leading down to
the river, to bathe or pray or float flower-
offerings downstream.

As Mani dressed, he heard the blare of
a bus horn. There was only the one bus to
Mussoorie. He scampered up the slope,
wondering if they'd miss it. But Granny
was waiting for him at the bus stop. She
had already bought their tickets.

Chapter Four

The motor-road followed the course of the
river, which thundered a hundred feet below.
The bus was old and rickety, and rattled so
much that the passengers could barely hear
themselves speaking. One of them was
pointing to a spot below, where another
bus had gone off the road a few weeks back.

The driver appeared to be unaware of the accident. He drove at some speed, and whenever he went round a bend, everyone in the bus was thrown about and luggage skidded about on the floor. In spite of all the noise and confusion, Granny fell asleep, her head resting against Mani's shoulder.

Suddenly the bus came to a grinding halt. People were thrown forward in their seats. Granny's glasses fell off and had to be retrieved from the folds of someone else's umbrella.

'What's happening?' she asked. 'Have we arrived?'

'No, something is blocking the road,' said Mani.

'It's a landslide!' exclaimed someone, and all the passengers put their heads out of the windows to take a look.

It was a big landslide. Sometime in the night, during the heavy rain, earth and trees and bushes had given way and come crashing down, completely blocking the road. Nor was it over yet. Debris was still falling. Mani saw rocks hurtling down the hill and into the river.

'*Not* a suitable place for a bus stop,' observed Granny, although she couldn't see a thing.

Even as she spoke, a shower of stones and small rocks came clattering down on the roof of the bus. Passengers cried out in alarm.

The driver began reversing the bus. More rocks came crashing down.

Chapter Five

'Did you bring any food from Raju Uncle's house?' asked Mani.

'Naturally,' said Granny. 'I knew you'd soon be hungry. There are pakoras and buns, and milk-sweets and peaches from your uncle's garden.'

'Good!' said Mani, forgetting his tiredness.

'We'll eat as we go along. There's no need to stop.'

'Eating or walking?'

'Eating, of course. We'll stop when you're tired, Granny.'

'Oh, I can walk for ever,' said Granny, laughing. 'I've been doing it all my life. And one day I'll just walk over the mountains and into the sky. But not if it's raining. This umbrella leaks badly.'

Down again they went, and up the next mountain, and through fields and over bare windswept hillsides, and up through a dark, gloomy deodar forest where a band of monkeys followed them until Mani gave them what was left of his pakoras. And then, just as it was getting dark, they saw the lights of Mussoorie twinkling ahead of them.

As they came nearer to the town, the lights

increased, until presently they were in a brightly-lit bazaar, swallowed up by crowds of shoppers, strollers, tourists and merry-makers. Mussoorie seemed a very jolly sort of place for those who had money to spend. Jostled in the crowds, Granny kept one hand firmly on Mani's shoulder so that she did not lose him.

They asked around for the cheapest hotel. But there were no cheap hotels. So they spent the night in a dharamsala adjoining the temple, where other pilgrims had taken shelter for the night.

Next morning, at the eye hospital, they joined a long queue of patients. The eye specialist, a portly man in a suit and tie who himself wore glasses, dealt with the patients in a brisk but kind manner.

After an hour's wait, Granny's turn came.

Chapter Six

The doctor took one horrified look at Granny's glasses and dropped them into a waste-paper basket.

Then he fished them out and placed them on his desk and said, 'On second thoughts, I think I'll send them to a museum. You should have changed them years ago. They've probably done more harm than good.'

He examined Granny's eyes with a strong light, and said, 'Your eyes are very weak, but you're not going blind. We'll fit you up with a stronger pair of glasses.'

Then he placed Granny in front of a board covered with letters in English and Hindi, large and small, and asked her if she could make them out.

'I can't even see the board,' said Granny.

'Well, can you see me?' asked the doctor.

'Some of you,' said Granny.

'I want you to see all of me,' said the doctor, and he balanced a wireframe on Granny's nose and began trying out different lenses.

Suddenly Granny could see much better. She saw the board and the biggest letters on it.

'Can you see me now?' asked the doctor.

'Most of you,' replied Granny. And then added, by way of being helpful: 'There's quite a lot of you to see.'

'Thank you,' said the doctor. 'And now turn around and tell me if you can see your grandson.'

Granny turned, and saw Mani clearly for the first time in many years.

'Mani!' she exclaimed, clapping her hands with joy. 'How nice you look! What a fine boy I've brought up! But you do need a haircut. And a wash. And buttons on your shirt. And a new pair of shoes. Come along to the bazaar!'

'First have your new glasses made,' said Mani, laughing. 'Then we'll go shopping!'

A day later they were in a bus again, although no one knew how far it would be able to go. Sooner or later they would have to walk.

Granny had a window seat, and Mani sat
beside her. He had new shoes and Granny had
a new umbrella, and they had also bought
a thick woollen Tibetan pullover for Mani's
father. And seeds and bulbs and a cowbell.

As the bus moved off, Granny looked
eagerly out of the window. Each bend in the
road opened up new vistas for her, and she
could see many things that she hadn't seen for

a long time—distant villages, people working in the fields, milkmen on the road, two dogs rushing along beside the bus, monkeys in the trees, and, most wonderful of all, a rainbow in the sky.

She couldn't see perfectly, of course . . . but she was very pleased with the improvement.

'What a large cow!' she remarked, pointing at a beast grazing on the hillside.

'It's not a cow, Granny,' said Mani. 'It's a buffalo.'

Granny was not to be discouraged. 'Anyway, I *saw* it,' she insisted.

While most of the people in the bus looked weary and bored, Granny continued to gaze out of the window, discovering new sights.

Mani watched for a time and listened to her excited chatter. Then his head began to nod. It dropped against Granny's shoulder, and remained there, comfortably supported. The bus swerved and jolted along the winding mountain road, but Mani was fast asleep.